# Goodnight Telluride

By Chris Beavers and Mary Storey

with illustrations by Ashton Rogers

Featuring Lula Belle
Lula Belle Productions, LLC

# ACKNOWLEDGMENTS

Ashton for her ability to capture the childlike wonder of Telluride in her illustrations.

◆ ◆ ◆

Abby for suggesting we incorporate caricatures of Lula Belle in every drawing.

◆ ◆ ◆

The amazing winter and summer experiences our family has had
in Telluride, which have overwhelmingly contributed to this book.

◆ ◆ ◆

Chloe, Rob and Jennifer for their guidance throughout this publishing process.

◆ ◆ ◆

There are countless worthy places and events that are part of the Telluride
experience that we were not able to include in this book. For this, we apologize.

All rights reserved. Published by Lula Belle Productions, LLC.
www.goodnightusa.com
Production date: November, 2014

Library of Congress Cataloging-in-Publication Data
Beavers, Chris
Storey, Mary

Goodnight Telluride, by Chris Beavers and Mary Storey;
illustrated by Ashton Rogers. ---- 1st ed.

For Ashton, Abby, Forrest, Alex and Mary Alden

Way up in the San Juan Mountains, at 9,000 feet,

Are happy little girls and boys drifting off to sleep!

Goodnight to all the silver gondolas
that carry us up and down.

Goodnight to Brown Dog Pizza! Telluride is a tasty pizza town!

Goodnight to
the Magic Carpet
where we learn to ski!

Goodnight to Enchanted Forest
with jumps, bumps and lots of trees!

Goodnight to Town Park,
with so many things to do.

Goodnight to wading in the river and riding inner tubes.

Goodnight to the snowboard park
where we catch some serious air!

Goodnight to all the goodies at Baked in Telluride!

Goodnight to EcoAdventures,
summer day camp
and bike rides!

Goodnight to Roudy
and all of his friendly horses.

Goodnight to the Peaks Hotel, with its spa, pool and golf courses.

Goodnight to "Between the Covers,"
the best ever bookstore!

Goodnight to the landmark
Sheridan Opera House
where we go for plays,
concerts and more!

Goodnight to Maggie's yummy pancakes for all ages!

Goodnight to festival goers rocking to music on big stages!

Goodnight to Ah Haa School for the Arts,
where artists learn to explore!

Goodnight to the biggest sky we have ever seen with moon and stars galore!

Goodnight to tons of toys and games at Zia Sun!

Goodnight to Elk Park with picnics,
hula hoops and fun! fun! fun!

Goodnight to Farmers' Market
with tasty treats in every stall!

Goodnight to speedy little prairie dogs
and elk roaming the Valley Floor.

Goodnight TELLURIDE!
We will definitely be back for more!

# WE OFFER SPECIAL THANKS TO:

Ashton for her awesome illustrations!

◆ ◆ ◆

Bud for his legal advice, support and generous spirit!

◆ ◆ ◆

Lula Belle for being such an amazing dog!

◆ ◆ ◆

Ashton, Abby, Forrest, Alex and Mary Alden
(Mary's grandchildren) for being our inspiration for this book!

◆ ◆ ◆

The Town of Telluride, CO, for thoughtfully protecting
and preserving this little piece of heaven!

◆ ◆ ◆

Telluride Ski and Golf for its investment in this beautiful,
unique region nestled in the San Juan Mountains.

◆ ◆ ◆

The People of Telluride for their love of this magical place!